T0380875

# *My great, great, Grandfather was <u>Not</u> a Fish*

## A STORY OF EVOLUTION

BY FRANK LATINO

ARTWORK BY ALEXANDRÉ R. LINO

WestBow Press books may be ordered through booksellers or by contacting:

WestBow Press
A Division of Thomas Nelson & Zondervan
1663 Liberty Drive
Bloomington, IN 47403
www.westbowpress.com
844-714-3454

Interior Image Credit: Alexandré Roesner Lino

ISBN: 978-1-9736-5016-4 (sc)
ISBN: 978-1-9736-5017-1 (e)

Library of Congress Control Number: 2019900028

Print information available on the last page.

WestBow Press rev. date: 12/04/2023

WESTBOW
PRESS®
A DIVISION OF THOMAS NELSON
& ZONDERVAN

# My great, great, Grandfather was <u>Not</u> a Fish

My great, great, grandfather was NOT a fish!

The *true story of Evolution

*Story according to Frank Latino

Artwork by Alexandre Roesner Lino

Note to the customer who
does buy this book…

Your child may be inquisitive and may ask
"how was the earth made?"
This narrative is what many illustrious scientists believe.

Many millions of miles far out in the universe, one of the stars, many million times bigger than our sun, started to expand, and swell, and tremor, and quake…

and then it exploded… A tremendous explosion that shattered this star into billions of segments that shot like rockets in every direction…

these burning 'molten rock' sections, 'globs' of all sizes, (we call them meteors), traveled through space at tremendous speeds. A large number of these flaming meteors traveled close enough to a planet to get caught up in that planet's gravitational pull, therefore it would crash into that planet.

The majority of these burning meteors continued their wild flight, spinning through space… Occasionally, we see a burning meteor speeding through space, and we refer to them as "shooting stars". A large number of these flaming meteors crashed into each other, and when that happened, (being melted burning rock, they were 'gooey') and they would 'stick' together, to form a larger meteor. These meteors were flaming melted rock, like lava from a volcano.

When a sizable group of these meteors stuck together, they formed an even larger meteor that now was big enough to have its own gravitational pull… (which is how at the earth began).

As more and more meteors 'crashed' into the earth, the earth got larger and larger, beginning to have the approximate shape of a ball. God made this all happen! God guided this ball into a perfect orbit around the sun, if it was closer, or further, the Earth would be too hot or cold for His plan.

My great, great, Grandfather was Not a fish!

My great, great grandfather was not a fish,
and if I could ever meet him, that's what I wish.

In Heaven, I'm sure he still is there,
and my hope, in Heaven, is what we'd share.

My great, great granddad, is really a unique man,
cause he was the first part, of God's special plan.
My friend, this is what I really do believe,
cause after Adam, God then made Eve.

Many, millions of years before, God made
all of the animals by the score, and then…

He really made, so many more. A fish is how God
did make his start, and with each change,
He gave them all… a different heart.

Now, it was the animals that did evolve, from a fish to an ape,
they changed their shape, and along with their guise, they
changed their size, even as wine does come, to us…from the
sweetest grape, these animals did change their size, and also
changed their shape, but every change these animals made,
it was because,

God's hand on them, that was surely laid.

Never confuse animals with man,
Atheists say: "man came from the Ape,
it just happened, there was no plan."
This thought of theirs, really does stink,
Because they have never found, and will never
find…that 'missing link'!

Now, friend, I want to make this, perfectly clear,
those foolish claims, please do not hear,
I'll tell you now, God's true, and special plan,
was all about how God did make a man…

God set man over animals, as this was
man's domain,
He never intended animals, and man,
to ever be the same.
God also gave man a conscience, and
his own free will, thus, he could be pure,
and good, or wicked, and garner much shame,
as it was…with Abel's brother…
you know…his name was Cain.

But good people, you can rejoice in joy, and glory,
because I know, this is, the absolute, sure,
and really true…evolution story:

God took this planet, that really was burning, and
slowed it down from the extreme speed,
that it was turning.

He cooled it off, and filled the oceans, with real cold water, then He put lots of fish in them, all sizes, and really different shapes, (well sorter).

Most all these fish just swam around,
but some jumped up… to see the ground.

So God asked them if they would like to go,
on… to the land, and they said:
"if we could…my God…that would be,
really…just so grand."
He told one fish you'll just have to jump up, a little bit
farther, if you want to get up… on to the land,

and that fish, did jump up, and then, he did go, and land,
on a beach…a beach, that was all full of sand.

Now this fish was on the ground…
but all he could do, was…'flip' around.

So God gave him, some legs, so he could walk around,
and that fish, with legs, suddenly found...
that he could get up... right off the ground.

Now, that fish with legs, did go, jump up, and ran
around, he danced, and danced, and even did a little jog,

and then when he tired, he went and rested … on a log,

and soon he became… a real cute,

a really cute,... little frog!

Now, in time, that frog, then became

a dog!

and, that little dog, did become a Hog,

and both of them, really coming…
from that fish, and that little Frog.

Now, that frog, then became the dog
and, that little dog, did become a Hog,
and both of them, really coming …
from that fish, and that little frog

This book is too small to show changes in
every animal, every case,
but, know that in time this also did take
place.

These transitions perhaps took ten billion
years, as we count, that is, me and you …
But to God, He can do it within the time that
the sky turns from black …

... to a pretty light blue.

And maybe God thought, it
might be funny, to make...

...a chicken,

...a lamb,

...a goat,

...a donkey,

...a monkey,

...and also a bunny.

The donkey sat down, and saw the
goat was chasing the bunny and the
lamb,
then they all hopped up, and in
circles, all of them ran.

Then God made a nice big horse,
and so on, and so on, 'cause this
was,
God's great idea, of course...

Some people may find this
story, is quite amusing,
while some may find it a little
bit confusing.
While others, may think
this tale is odd,
the real truth is...every word...
and every thought, that's
here... really does come from
God!
If you came in, a bit too late,
please stay,
and I will...
just for you...
re-iterate.
re-it-ter-ate, is such a big word,

*but it simply means… to repeat…*
*So this story now… I will repeat, because*
*this tale, you'll hear… is really is so very neat.*
*So, this fish first became a frog, and then a dog,*
*and then a hog…then a chicken, a lamb, a goat, a monkey, a donkey, a funny bunny, or maybe even a horse, and so on, and so on, because this was*
*God's great idea, of course.*

When God made the donkey, and
monkey, God thought the monkey
could lose that tail, and even have a
bigger shape, so then He decided…
to make an Ape, as this was
also part of His great Plan…

'cause after that Ape...God then
made...
His first... brand new man!

To view this man, God made him
twirl,
and then pleased with man, God
then…
for this man… He made…

...a really pretty girl!
So now, you know, and you can
surely believe,
that man was Adam, and that
pretty girl,
...was Eve!

Then God was now, to lead them…
right into
His beautiful… and special
…garden, of Eden.

So God made it all… every rock, all the
grass,
and every tree…and He helped that fish
swim, …then jump up, right out of the sea.
Evolution did not happen…all by itself,
it could never happen, without God's help.
As God helped them all to evolve… some did
come out, well, kind of strange… so it was
up to God…
it was His problem to correct, or solve…and
then,
when He did… He made them all change!
So if God did not help that fish to
jump up, right onto the ground, we all
would
still be, in that big sea, just swimming
around!

Maybe we would be, as small as a minnow,
or as large, as the biggest, white whale,
but this is for sure…we only would only be
able
to swim around… with our scaly, fish tail!
We should all thank God for His wonderful
world,
and, for His marvelous, and tremendous
plan,
whether He made us into a beautiful girl…
or as
He… in His own image… made us into,
a real good looking man!

"Dear Reader,
I hope this book has told you about matters,
that perhaps, you never knew,
but I promise you,
The facts that's told here, in my opinion,
are really, so very true.
As I hope your sky,
always stays a lovely, clear bright blue,
I pray that God will now, and forever,
place His blessings right on you,
and Now, the time has come,
when we must say goodbye, my friend,
when we must part, because sadly
to say this, but we have now come
to the end...the very end!"